LARGE PRINT

Bedtime Stories

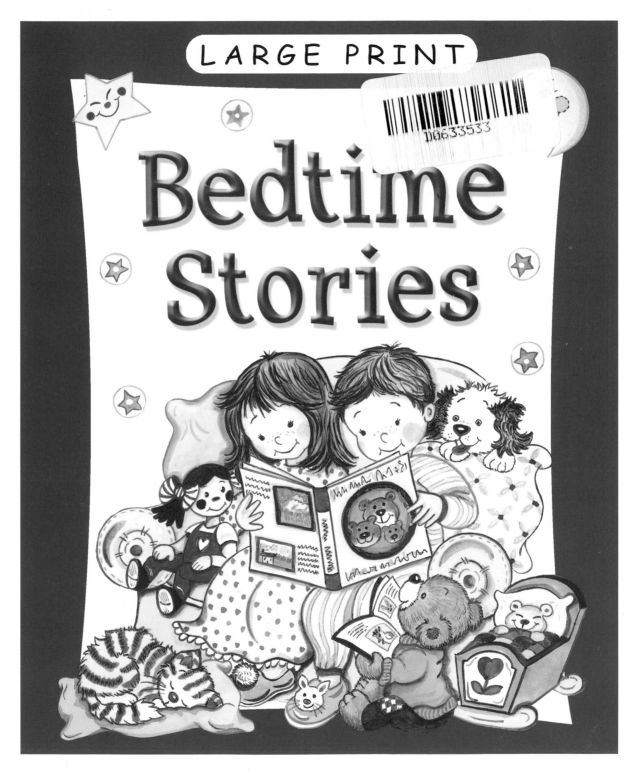

Brown Watson

ENGLAND

On the Farm

Betty, the cow, had been at Green Fields Farm for as long as anyone could remember. Even Farmer Smith could not say when it was that he brought her back from the market to lead the herd.

"Where this farm would be without me, I just don't know," she was fond of saying. "I'm so important!"

"We all work very hard, too!" Billy Goat would protest.

But Betty never tired of telling how important she was.

Betty was also very nosey, snooping around, trying to see what the other animals were doing, hoping to pass on any gossip to Farmer Smith. And, if there was nothing to tell him, she would make things up!

"I see Mother Horse was late out of the stables once again this morning. Maybe she's feeling ill, poor old thing. More work for me, I suppose, doing her job, making sure the foal doesn't wander off."

"I was waiting for the blacksmith to fit my new shoes!" cried Mother Horse when Farmer Smith asked her why she was late starting work. "Did you forget he was calling today? Betty did say she would remind you!"

But Betty always had an answer!
"I can't remember everything," she would say.
But she could remember all that she wanted to tell Farmer Smith – whether he wanted to hear it, or not!

"Baa-Baa let her friend lead the flock this afternoon!"
"Billy Goat ate some pig feed!"
"Mother Hen slept for hours!"
"Sally the dog cut her paw! She won't be fit for work tomorrow, I'm sure of it!"

"Yes, I will!" barked Sally. "I only went across the raspberry patch to fetch one of Baa-Baa's lambs!"
But, of course, Betty did not tell Farmer Smith that. He was very angry to think that Sally had been careless.

"We must do something about Betty's tale-telling," clucked old Mother Hen. "But if we do say anything," bleated Billy, "she'll go to Farmer Smith." "Maybe," said Sally, "that could be just what we want..."

Betty was most interested to hear the animals talking so seriously together in the barn.
"It's hidden in the raspberry patch!" Sally the dog was saying. "Nobody will ever find it."

"Find what?" asked Betty at once. "What's in the raspberry patch?"
"Raspberry patch?" said Sally.
"Raspberry patch?" echoed Baa-Baa.
"Raspberry patch?" said Billy. "What about the raspberry patch?"

Next morning, Betty began searching, nosing around the raspberry patch, determined to find whatever was hidden in there.

"Where's Betty?" thundered Farmer Smith. "She's late for milking!"

"Oh, Farmer Smith," began Betty, "I've been so busy! I ----" But he had already stormed off in a temper.
"See you later," she heard Baa-Baa calling to Billy. "It's my turn to go to the raspberry patch."

"Not if I get there first!" Betty said to herself, determined to get to the raspberry patch before Baa-Baa and start searching again. "The little beasts! Fancy them having a secret and not telling me!"

But after lots more nosing around, still Betty found nothing.

"Ooh!" she burst out. "If only I could find out exactly what's hidden!"

So, off she marched to the stables. Nobody was there.

She went to the barn – but nobody was there, either. Everywhere seemed so quiet – except for what sounded like a sudden burst of laughter from behind the hedge. Betty gave the most loud, most furious moo.

"The raspberry patch! They've waited until my back was turned so that they could go and get their treasure from the raspberry patch!" Off she went. When she reached the raspberry patch, there was nobody there either.

By now, Betty was in a fine, old temper, nosing around among the raspberries with even more fury.

Then a voice thundered, "Betty! What on earth are you playing at? It's long past milking time, again!"

"Those animals," said Betty, "they have hidden something here, and I mean to find it!"
The last thing she expected was for the farmer to throw back his head and laugh, as if he would never be able to stop!

"Come with me and take a look in the duck pond," he spluttered at last. "First time in my life I have ever seen a pink-nosed cow!"

"Pink-nosed cow?" screamed Betty, almost running to keep up with him.

"Now you can see what a fine nose you really have!" bleated Billy Goat, loud enough for Farmer Smith to hear. "Just right for being nosey!" Baa-Baa chimed in.

"Soon see you coming!" added Hen.

Poor Betty! The juice from the ripe, red raspberries had turned her nose bright pink! She looked so sorry for herself that Farmer Smith began laughing again, and this time all the animals joined in.

How Betty wished she had never listened to the animals talking about the raspberry patch. But you may be sure, that by the time her pink nose faded, she had made up her mind never to be nosey again!

The Little Motor Car

Maurice the motor car had once been the smartest car on the road. His headlamps shone, his windows sparkled and his paintwork gleamed.

Whether it was an outing to the seaside or picnics in the summer, parties or trips into town in the winter, everyone was always so pleased to see him.

But when he began getting rusty and his seats started to sag, Maurice was sold to a man who mended motorbikes. He kept what he called his "bits and pieces" on the back seat.

Then came the day when the man bought a brand new van.

"Grandad will be having you, Maurice" he said. "Your gears creak and your engine wheezes, but you won't be going far from now on."

Maurice tried very hard not to mind
too much.
But all too soon, the old man could
no longer drive him around, and he
was dumped in the corner of a scrap
yard down the road.
Poor Maurice! All he could see were
old washing machines, worn-out tyres
and every sort of rubbish you can
think of. There was nothing to do,
nobody to talk to.

Being out in the rain meant he quickly got rustier than ever. Then, suddenly, his roof started to leak.

"Surely," old Maurice thought, "nobody could hate rain more than me!" But, he was wrong....

Maurice was so miserable, cold and tired, he hardly noticed two little mice paying him a visit. They needed to shelter inside for a very special reason....

The two little mice were soon busy, chewing up bits of paper blown in by the wind and tearing strips of rag to weave with some of Maurice's back seat. He didn't mind, at all!

Maurice soon guessed that something exciting was about to happen, the way the two mice kept chattering and squeaking to each other. He could hardly believe he had so many new friends, all at once!

And the mice were not the only ones who decided to make their home with Maurice. The moment sharp-eyed Mrs. Robin saw the old car, she knew that was where she wanted her nest.

With a family of robins singing so sweetly all day and the lively mice scampering around and playing in their nice little home, Maurice decided he had never been happier!

Then, one morning, everything changed.
No birds sang, no mice squeaked and
chattered. Surely, Maurice told himself, his
friends would not have left him so
suddenly? But, they had.

Maurice felt so sad. He was still trying to think what could have happened, when he heard a tiny cry coming from the front seat. It sounded just like a tiny kitten, mewing!

"So that's why the mice and the robins left so suddenly," smiled Maurice to himself, knowing how frightened they would be with a cat around.

As for the kittens, it was plain they loved being with Maurice. When they were not playing together outside, he could hear them purring as they slept underneath the steering wheel.

The only thing that worried him was the thought of the kittens growing up. Would they leave him then, he wondered? Already they were wandering further and further away – Mother Cat, as well....

The family to which Maurice had once belonged now seemed so far away, it was quite a shock to hear footsteps and a voice calling out: "Hey, come here everybody! See who I've found!"

"It's Tabitha!" cried a little girl. Maurice could see her stroking the Mother Cat's furry head.

"We told you we'd seen her near here, didn't we, Daddy? Robert was sure she'd had her kittens."

"And I was right!" shouted her brother, climbing into Maurice's driving seat. "Lucky she found this old car! Isn't it great, Amy?" "Honk–honk!" Amy was much too busy, sounding the horn. "Honk–honk!"

Robert and Amy played for a long time with Maurice. He could tell they did not really want to go home, not even when their Daddy called: "Come along, you two! Tabitha's new family is waiting!"

"We wouldn't mind having the car too!" Maurice heard Robert saying. His Daddy laughed – but what was said next, Maurice didn't know. By the next day, he was so sad, he hardly cared what happened to him.

"Here's the old banger!" said a voice,
breaking into Maurice's thoughts. "Engine
and gear-box out, right?"
"Right!" came the reply. "Must be a spare
parts job, I reckon."

"Spare parts!" echoed Maurice. "Don't say I'm to be broken up!" But when his tyres were levered off one by one, and a crane hauled him high into the air, he knew it must be true.

Maurice shut his eyes tight. It seemed nobody wanted him any more. But, when he opened them again, what do you think? There were loud cheers from the back seat!

"Good old Daddy!" he heard Robert shout. "He knew we needed the car for the adventure playground, Amy!" But Amy was far too busy swinging on one of Maurice's old tyres!

The Witch and the Cat

What's your idea of a witch's cat?
A cat like me, perhaps — black, with
sharp, pointed ears, big eyes and a
long tail? And the witch? Well, you
probably wouldn't expect her to be
forgetful and stupid, getting into all
sorts of muddles and screaming
"Willow!" at the sight of a mouse —
would you?

But then, you probably don't know my mistress, Wumpet the Witch! I heard her say once that she got her name from a spell which had gone wrong.... And, with Wumpet around, that's nothing unusual!

"Wee-wee-willow-wickety.... er.... Wicky-won-wackety..." (Wumpet has never ever quite managed to remember the right words for a spell, yet!) "Or, is it Winny-wack-williby?" No wonder her magic gets all mixed up!

I can usually see when spells are starting to go wrong, long before Wumpet does. That's how it is that I always manage to get out of the way in time, and she doesn't!

But, whether I hide under the stairs, or up in the attic, Wumpet is never far away! So you can guess how pleased I was to find a hole in the fence, just big enough for me to squeeze through.

"Hello," said a voice, not a bit like Wumpet's. "You're the cat from next door, aren't you?"

Without thinking, I mewed at her, "Yes, that's right," hoping that she would understand. And, she did!

What's more, she seemed to know about Wumpet, too.

"I've seen you with that silly old witch," she said and stroked my head.

"Would you like one of my cheese crackers?"

Cheese crackers! I had never tasted cheese crackers in my whole life! Then she brought me a saucer of rich, creamy milk and an old blanket, in case I wanted to lie down.

"Don't forget that cat belongs to someone else," came another voice.

Jenny laughed. "He is just like a friend come round to play, Mummy. That's all right, isn't it?"

And, so it was. Jenny never once said a word about Wumpet, or about me being a witch's cat. That was just one of our little secrets. If Wumpet only knew how we laughed at her.

And what with all the snacks Jenny kept feeding me, I was getting fatter and fatter – which meant the hole in the fence got bigger and bigger, until even Wumpet could see it.

Of course, I squeezed back through the hole as quickly as I could, but it was too late!

"So!" she screeched in her loud, witchy sort of voice. "This is where you go when my back is turned, eh?"

She stamped back indoors, and came out
waving a rolling-pin!
"My magic wand!" she said with a wild
cackle. "Now I can get one of my spells
working on this."
Jenny and I held our breath.

She straightened her pointed hat and
began to sing.
"Minny-mon-moony. Cold ginger beer!
Great big hole, please disappear!"
Then, she turned round three times.

Poor old Wumpet! She didn't realise she had holes in her skirt and her magic made the holes disappear, until there was no skirt left! But the hole in the fence was still as big as it had ever been....

Next day, we watched Wumpet dragging out her cauldron.
"Magic potion!" she kept puffing to herself.
"That's what I need!" She gave a snort in our direction, but we pretended not to notice.

"Dandelion and daisy root! Lollipop sticks and football boot! Hair of maggot, slice of rain! Put my fence to rights, again!" It seemed that this time, Wumpet had actually got the words right for once!

And can you guess what happened next? Nothing at all! All day long and half the night Wumpet kept on with that spell, getting angrier and angrier. The words became more muddled each time.

"Wonder what she's going to do next?" said Jenny. She was trying hard not to laugh out loud, but it wasn't easy – not when we could see Wumpet getting tangled up in armfuls of long twigs and more spell books!

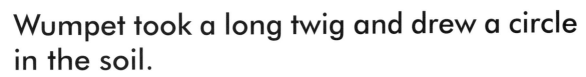

Wumpet took a long twig and drew a circle in the soil.

"Circle and square, drawn here today, please make the hole in the fence go away!"

"Drat!" she shouted. "Drat, drat!"

"Is that part of the spell?" Jenny and I giggled helplessly.

"Drat!" Wumpet screamed again. "I forgot to dip the stick in the juice of a red jelly-bean! I'll have to go and fetch one!"

By now, Jenny was laughing so much that her Daddy came out to see what was happening.

"Er, it's the cat from next door," said Jenny hastily. "He looks so funny, squeezing through the fence."

"Yes, Mummy did mention it. I'll fetch my tools, Jenny, then we can patch it up with a bit of wood and some nails. I don't suppose the old lady next door has even noticed it," he remarked, as he started to saw and hammer.

When Wumpet came out again and saw that the fence had been mended, she gave a whoop of delight. "My magic worked, after all!" she cackled. "One of my best spells! Kippers for tea tonight, Willow!"